TIMMIE IN PARIS

Timmie in Paris

BY VIVIAN WERNER

illustrated by Elise Piquet

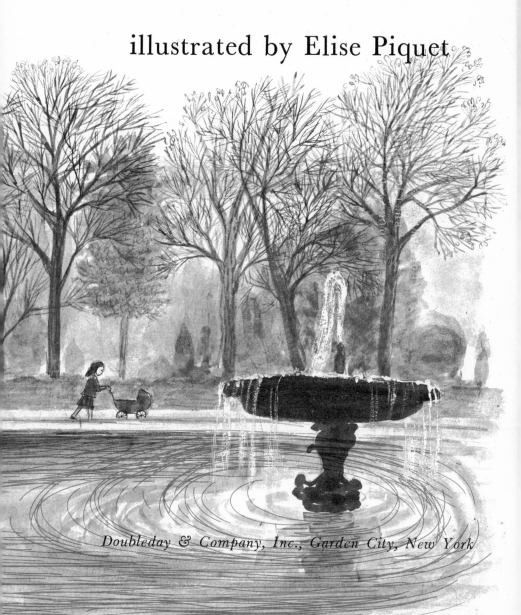

Doubleday & Company, Inc., Garden City, New York

Library of Congress Catalog Card Number 65-19937
Text Copyright © 1965 by Vivian Werner
Illustrations Copyright © 1965 by Elise Piquet
All Rights Reserved
Printed in the United States of America
First Edition

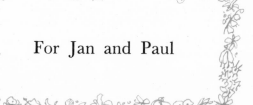

For Jan and Paul

CONTENTS

TIMMIE IN PARIS

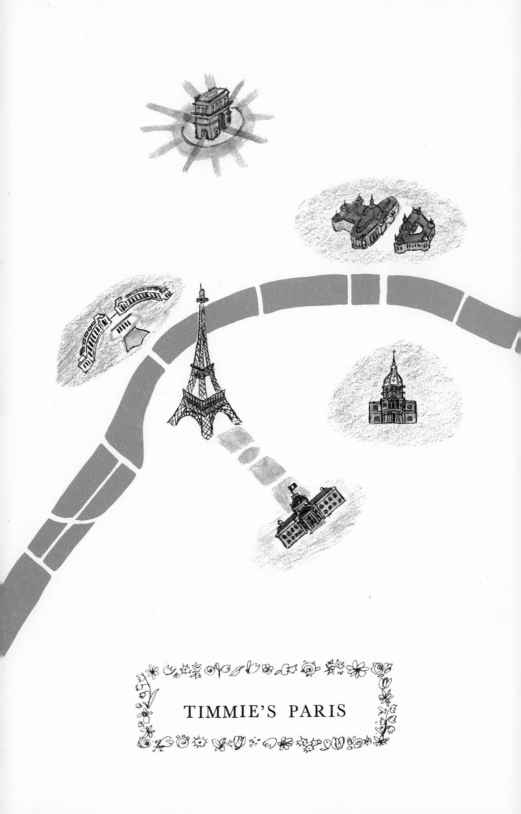

TIMMIE'S PARIS

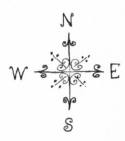

1

. . . in Paris

Everything was different.

To begin with, the way people talked was different.

When the maid with the breakfast tray (and even *that* was different) knocked on the door, she didn't say "Good morning" the way anyone at home would.

She said "Bonjour" (*bo nzhoor*). And then she smiled at Timmie. So Timmie smiled back and said "Bonjour," too, and then he was very proud of himself because he was speaking French, his very first day in Paris.

Breakfast was different, too.

Timmie could hardly remember a single day when he didn't start off with a glass of orange juice, back home. And after that, he had oatmeal or corn flakes or bacon and eggs. And of course, Sunday mornings, he *always* had pancakes with great melting blobs of butter, and the little blue pitcher full of maple syrup.

But this morning, he didn't have any of those.

Instead, Timmie had a whole pitcher full of hot chocolate that he drank from a huge, heavy, white cup, while Mother and Daddy had coffee with milk in it that they called "café au lait" (*caffay oh lay*). With it, they all had rolls as flaky as pie crust and as melting as the cotton candy Timmie ate on Fair Day.

The rolls were shaped like the new moon, and when Timmie asked what they were, Mother said they were "croissants" (*krwahsnt*).

Timmie ate them with little curls of sweet yellow butter and a pot full of strawberry jam. They were so delicious that Timmie ate five.

They were so delicious that Timmie would have eaten more—six or seven, perhaps—but of course, he didn't want to seem greedy.

Now Timmie stood in front of the long window that reached all the way from the ceiling to the floor. Down below him was the Boulevard and what Mother called "Paris traffic." To Timmie, it looked just like New York traffic. Timmie knew all about New York traffic because he and Mother and Daddy had spent two days there before they took the plane that brought them to France.

Still, Mother said, "Paris traffic! Honestly!"

Whatever Mother thought of Paris traffic, Timmie found it fun to watch. From the window, he could see tiny cars weaving in and out and speeding to the corner and stopping suddenly and starting again with a hump and a jump.

Timmie thought at first that the cars seemed tiny because he was up so high. Then it seemed to him that they were awfully small, anyway. They seemed to be just his size. So Timmie asked Mother if he could go down to look at them up close. When she said "Yes, dear, but be very careful," Timmie went down the hall to the elevator. He pushed the bell, but the elevator didn't come. He rang again and waited.

Then Timmie remembered that Daddy said most elevators in Paris only went *up*. Timmie thought that was very silly. If it went up, it must come down, too.

But it certainly wasn't coming down for *him*.

So Timmie ran down the three flights of stairs that twisted around the elevator shaft like the stripes on a candy cane.

He pushed open the heavy hotel door and rushed

over to the curb. And then he just stood and stared.

He had been right!

Some of the cars really *were* tiny. Just little-boy-size! No taller than Timmie, and not much longer than his big red wagon at home.

There were little gray cars made half of canvas and half of tin. And little blue cars and little black cars, too. Timmie could see right over the tops of them all.

There were sport cars, too, even lower than the others—red, yellow, and green ones—just big enough for two people.

And bicycles! Right in the middle of all the traffic!

And motorcycles darting in front of the little cars, and getting away just in time. Timmie was so sure there'd be a smashup, he held his breath.

Then a big bus came lumbering by. It was very old and Timmie thought it must be tired because it moved so slowly. The bus had a platform at the back where a lot of people stood, right out in the open air.

That was where Timmie wanted to ride.

He stepped back a little bit away from the curb,

because all the cars and the bicycles and the motor scooters were going so fast. He stepped back and stood watching until a long, low, cream-colored car with the top down came streaking by. That, Timmie decided, was just the kind of car he would buy, when he was a man.

He leaned against a tree and looked up. Overhead, the sky was as blue as the blanket on his bed at home. The buildings seemed blue, too, but a different kind of blue, that was partly gray and partly silver.

Above Timmie the trees caught the sunlight in their pale green leaves and tossed it back and forth before they let it fall to the ground.

When Timmie grew tired of watching the leaves, he made up a little game. He ran over to the sidewalk to a patch of sunlight. Then he tried to leap over the shadows, to jump from one sunny patch to the next. He was so busy trying not to step on the shady spots that he didn't even notice where he was going.

And in just a few minutes, Timmie turned the corner.

He went on, hopping along the sidewalk, until he was halfway down the block.

Suddenly Timmie stopped.

There, at the next corner, was a big stone building with a high stone wall around it. Timmie couldn't see over the wall, but he could hear squeals and squeaks and chattering from inside it. From the noise, Timmie knew there would be other children there.

He rushed down the rest of the block and stopped in front of two big iron grillwork doors. Over the doorway was carved the word "Ecole" which Timmie knew was pronounced *ay-cole*. He knew, too, that it meant "school." And inside, flying from the top of

the building, Timmie could see a blue, white, and red flag.

Through the grillwork, Timmie peeped into the schoolyard. He saw that it was full of little girls, playing and running about and chasing one another.

They reminded him of the little girls he played with at home, Betty and Sally and Laura. But these little girls weren't wearing blue jeans, like the little girls at home. And they weren't wearing the stiffly starched dresses that Betty and Sally and Laura wore when they got dressed up.

These little girls all wore smocks, like the kind

21

Timmie had seen painters wear in pictures. Some were red and some were green, and some of them were checked, and they all had big pockets with apples or oranges or bunches of grapes stitched on them. And all the smocks had long sleeves, that buttoned at the wrist.

Timmie stood and watched the little girls. He thought it would be fun to go in and play with them. But before he could make up his mind to do it, the little girls came streaming out of the yard, tumbling over one another and hurrying along the sidewalk.

None of them noticed Timmie.

Then when the schoolyard was almost empty and
Timmie was almost ready to go home, a little girl
with straight yellow hair and big brown eyes came
out of the building.

She was just Timmie's age—just eight years old.

She was just Timmie's size, too.

She didn't see Timmie until she reached the gate.

Then, as soon as she *did* see him, she rushed over
to him.

Timmie remembered the word he had learned
that morning. "Bonjour," he said politely.

The little girl giggled. Then she stuck out her
hand. "Bonjour," she said.

Timmie held out his hand, too.

The little girl took it and shook it, just once.

Just one quick, downward jerk. Not up-and-down, up-and-down, up-and-down, the way Timmie shook hands in America.

Just one quick, downward jerk.

"Je m'appelle Isabelle" (*zhuh mappelle Isabelle*), the little girl said.

And Timmie understood her. "*My* name is Timmie," he said.

Then Isabelle let go of Timmie's hand and ran back to the school building. When she came back, she was carrying a brief case like the kind Daddy had. She opened the brief case and took out a piece of bread and then a piece of chocolate.

The bread was different, too, from the kind Timmie had always eaten.

It was long and thin, and the crust was hard and golden-brown, and Timmie had never seen a piece of bread with so *much* crust.

Isabelle broke the chocolate in half and then she broke the bread in half and she handed a piece of each to Timmie.

Timmie didn't know what to say. He didn't know how to say "Thank you" in French, so he said it in English. "Thank you."

And then he smiled at Isabelle and she smiled back. "Pas de quoi" (*paw d' kwah*), she said. "You're welcome."

Timmie watched Isabelle and he did just what she did. He put his piece of chocolate right on top of the bread and then he bit into it. The chocolate was sweet and the bread was salty and the crust of the bread was chewy like a caramel. Timmie hadn't eaten anything so delicious since breakfast time.

When they had both finished munching their bread and chocolate, Isabelle ran away, down the street.

Timmie watched until she was gone.

Then he turned around and started back to the hotel.

He was very happy and he sang as he skipped along.

He had found a friend.

2

In the Park

When Timmie got back to the hotel, he didn't bother to take the elevator. He rushed up the stairs and dashed into the room to find Mother and Daddy and tell them all about Isabelle.

Mother and Daddy were very pleased. "Why, Timmie," they said, "you've made a friend."

Then Timmie asked Mother and Daddy how to say "thank you" in French.

"Merci" (*mairsee*), Mother said.

And Timmie said it after Mother, just the way she had. "Merci."

"And you ought to learn how to say 'please,' too," Mother said. "It's 's'il vous plaît'" (*seel voo play*).

So Timmie said, "S'il vous plaît," after Mother, and then he practiced saying it the rest of the day.

The next morning, when Mother asked Timmie if he'd like another croissant, he said "S'il vous plaît," and then, when Mother smiled and passed one to him, he said, "Merci."

Mother was delighted that Timmie was learning French so fast.

After breakfast, Mother suggested that Timmie might like to go out and find Isabelle again. So Timmie went skipping down the stairs and up the block to the school.

But he didn't hear any noise and he didn't see any children.

At first he thought that the little girls were still indoors.

He waited and waited and waited.

He waited almost five minutes.

But no one came and finally Timmie turned around and went home. He couldn't understand why there were no children at the school. He was sure it wasn't Saturday. He tried awfully hard to remember just what day it was. It wasn't Saturday and it wasn't Friday and Timmie was sure it must be Thursday.

And if it was Thursday, where was Isabelle?

Timmie hurried home to ask Mother.

And Mother said, "But of course, Timmie. I forgot. This is Thursday. French schools are closed on Thursday."

That seemed silly to Timmie, too, but he just shrugged his shoulders, the way he saw French people do, and decided to play by himself.

By lunchtime, though, Timmie was bored.

He'd read all the books he'd brought to Paris and he'd watched the cars from the window and he'd played with the building set Daddy had brought him.

He couldn't think of a single thing to do.

After lunch, Timmie said, "Mother, I don't have a single thing to do."

And Mother said, "But, Timmie! There are lots of things to do."

"What?" Timmie asked.

"Well," Mother said, and she thought for a minute, "you could read your books . . ."

"I've read them all," Timmie said.

". . . or watch the cars from the window . . ."

"I'm tired of doing that."

". . . or play with the nice building set Daddy brought you . . ."

"I'm tired of that, too," Timmie said.

Even Mother couldn't think of anything else for Timmie to do.

But Timmie could. "Why don't you teach me French?" he asked.

"Oh, Timmie darling," Mother said. Timmie was sure that meant "no." "I can't right now. I've got some things that just *have* to be done."

"I could help you!" Timmie declared.

"Oh, Timmie! I'm afraid not. These are grown-up things!"

Mother must have seen how disappointed Timmie

was, because she said, very quickly, "I know what you can do. You can go down to the pastry shop on the corner and pick out any cake you want."

At first Timmie thought he wouldn't know how to ask for a cake, but Mother just laughed and said, "All you have to do is point."

Then she gave him a crisp piece of paper that she called "French francs" and told him it was French money and sent him off.

Timmie hadn't gone more than halfway down the block when he saw Isabelle again. He knew her at once, and he went up to her and held out his hand and said "Bonjour" and smiled.

Isabelle smiled back.

Timmie wanted Isabelle to go to the pastry shop with him. He wanted to buy a cake for her, too. So he pointed toward the corner, but Isabelle shook her head and said "Non" (*nohn*) and pointed the other way.

Timmie wasn't sure where Isabelle wanted to go, but he took her hand anyway, and they walked off together down the street.

It wasn't long before they came to a huge park. It was fenced in, like the schoolyard, but at the gate there were little stands where old women with shawls around their shoulders were selling all sorts of wonderful things.

They were selling red and blue and yellow and green balloons, and some of them were shaped like

ducks and some were shaped like rabbits and some
of them had nets around them and little baskets
underneath and little French flags on the top.

The women were selling little boats, too, with little
white sails. And they were selling big, round, wooden
hoops, like the ones Timmie could see other children
rolling down the paths of the park.

Timmie wanted to stop and buy something, but
Isabelle ran on.

Timmie followed her past the big, bright beds of
flowers, past the stone building that must have been
a palace once, and past policemen standing in red-
white-and-blue striped houses that were just big
enough for one.

Isabelle ran on until she came to a large pond at

one end of the gardens. It was like the goldfish pool in Timmie's backyard at home, only much larger.

In the center of the pool was a fountain that spouted water high in the air, like the whale in Timmie's animal book. But this wasn't a picture at all. This was real and Timmie could feel the drops of water that sprayed on him when the wind blew his way.

And on the pond, best of all, were millions and millions—well, Timmie counted twenty-seven—of toy boats, with big white sails that puffed out in the breeze, and slid proudly across the water from one side to the other.

"Oh!" Timmie said. He stopped stock-still to watch.

It seemed to Timmie that the most exciting thing in the world would be to sail one of those boats on that pond. It would be more exciting than flying an airplane or going to the circus or eating a whole gallon of chocolate ice cream.

He stood there, wondering if he could sail a boat like that sometime and he said, "Oh!" once again, and then Isabelle tugged at his hand and pulled him along the path to a small cart that was loaded with boats just like the ones on the water.

Standing beside the cart was a man, and he was wearing a smock, too.

Isabelle dug into her pocket and held out some coins to the man. He took the money and then he took one of the boats from the cart and placed it in Isabelle's arms. He gave her a long pole and then she stepped back and waited.

And Timmie stepped forward and pointed to the most beautiful boat of all and held out the money Mother had given him, and the man put the boat in Timmie's arms and then he fished around in his pocket and gave lots of funny little coins back to Timmie, and then he handed him a pole, too.

Timmie ran off with the little ship and dropped it
into the water with a tremendous splash. Then he
shoved it with his pole. He shoved so hard he almost
fell in. But he caught his balance just in time and
the boat sailed off across the pond, and Timmie ran
around after it, and when he and the boat both
reached the other side, he shoved again and the boat
swung around and sailed back.

Timmie was halfway around the pond for the
hundred and eleventh time when he heard a sound
he had never heard before.

Ker-lump . . . ker-lump . . . ker-lump . . .

And when he looked up, Timmie saw a whole

caravan of little ponies and little donkeys plodding along the path.

Some of them had hats on their heads and ribbons around their ears, and a little brown donkey and a little brown pony were pulling a little wicker cart and in the cart were two little boys, just Timmie's age.

There were other boys and girls riding on the other little ponies, too, and a little gray donkey trotted along behind the others with no one on his back.

"Oh!" Timmie said. He rushed around the pond and found Isabelle and pointed to the cart. "Oh!" he said again.

And Isabelle nodded in excitement and said "Mais oui" (*meh wee*).

Then, together, Timmie and Isabelle ran after the ponies and the donkeys and the cart until it stopped beside a little booth where an old woman was selling tickets. Timmie went up to her and held out some money in one hand and with the other he held up two fingers.

"Deux?" (*duh*) the old woman asked.

Timmie pointed to Isabelle and then to himself.

"Deux," the old woman said. "Deux billets" (*duh bee-yeh*). And then she pushed two tickets through the tiny window.

Timmie scooped up the tickets, took Isabelle by the hand, and the two of them clambered up onto the little cart.

Then the brown donkey and the brown pony and all the others—even the little gray one—started off.

Ker-lump . . . *ker-lump* . . . *ker-lump* they went, jiggling and joggling along the path that went around the garden behind the little lake.

Isabelle was so happy that she laughed out loud, and then, when the donkey and the pony stepped faster and hurried around a curve and the cart went *bumpity-bumpity-bimpity-bump-bimp,* she squealed and grabbed Timmie's hand and held on very tight.

Timmie and Isabelle were still riding in the little cart when they heard a bell ringing.

As soon as she heard it, Isabelle laughed again. "Guignol!" (*geen-yol*) she said.

Timmie didn't understand her. So she said it again. "Guignol!" And this time she clapped her hands.

Even before the donkey cart stopped, Isabelle jumped off and ran down the path.

Timmie hopped down after her and scurried along until he caught up with her. Then he took her hand and they ran off together until they came to a medium-size building in the very middle of the big park.

Isabelle bought tickets and then she took Timmie's hand and pulled him inside and they had gone all the way to the front of the room before Timmie saw that he was in a theater and that the theater was full of children.

But he hardly had time to look around him before Isabelle had pushed him onto a seat on a bench in the front row and said "Guignol!" once more.

Then the lights went out and a little puppet in a little brown smock and with a black beret on his wooden head appeared in front of the red velvet curtains. "Bonjour!" the puppet said.

"Bonjour!" Timmie and the children shouted back.

And then the curtains opened and

40

Timmie saw lots and lots of puppets. Some were ladies in beautiful old-fashioned dresses that Timmie thought Mother would like to wear. And some were gentlemen with white wigs on their heads and long, curling feathers in their hats.

And then there was a dragon—a big, slinky, curling, coiling, speckled and spotted green creature—who opened his mouth and breathed out fire.

He frightened some of the children. But he didn't frighten Timmie.

Even if Timmie was only eight years old, he was *very* brave. But when the dragon captured the beautiful lady and took her off to his cave, Timmie was awfully glad that Isabelle was holding his own hand.

41

But then the hero, Guignol, came back, and, like Timmie, he wasn't *really* afraid of anything.

Guignol was so brave that he went right into the cave after the dragon. And he killed the dragon and rescued the beautiful lady, and everyone was so happy they all danced on the stage—all the beautiful ladies and the gentlemen with their white curls and their big, plumed hats, and even a whole ballet of green frogs.

It wasn't until after the show was over and Timmie and Isabelle were walking through the park once more that Timmie remembered Mother had given him money to buy a cake.

And Timmie only remembered it then, when, right in front of him, he saw a little house that looked just like the gingerbread house where Hansel and Gretel had found the old witch. But there wasn't a witch in *this* house, of course.

There was a jolly old lady with white hair who was baking waffles for the children who thronged around her.

Timmie walked right up to her and said, "Deux, s'il vous plaît." She baked two more, and while Timmie and Isabelle watched, she took them off the stove and sprinkled them with sugar and handed one to Isabelle and one to Timmie.

And Timmie and Isabelle ran off through the park, munching and crunching them.

They didn't stop until they came to a merry-go-round, just three bites and a chew away.

Timmie helped Isabelle climb onto a camel, and he climbed onto a giraffe. And off they went, round and round, while the music played.

Then, when at last they were beginning to get tired, they both jumped down and started home.

But before they left the park, and when one of the policemen turned around and couldn't see, Isabelle reached out her hand and plucked a whole fistful of flowers to take home.

43

After, they walked along slowly, until they came to the very place where Timmie had met Isabelle. Then she stopped and very gravely shook his hand just one short shake, and then she said "Au revoir" (*ohr vwahr*). Timmie knew that meant "good-by" so he said "Au revoir," too.

Then Isabelle trudged off down the block. But Timmie turned around and ran all the way home.

He was so excited that he ran all the way up the stairs, too, and into Mother's room. And then of course, he told Mother everything he'd done.

And Mother said, "Why, Timmie. You've been to the Luxembourg Gardens."

3

To Market, to Market

One morning, Timmie and Mother were walking along the Boulevard together when Timmie spied something in a window. It was big and round and white, with feathers, and he thought it was a lampshade.

But Mother said it was a hat. "A Paris hat!" was exactly what she said. "And isn't it beautiful!"

Timmie still thought it looked like a lampshade, and he started to giggle.

But Mother insisted it was a hat, and then she said, "I think I'll just go in and try it on."

So Timmie took Mother's hand and they went into the little shop together.

"That hat in the window," Mother said to the saleslady. "The white one with the feathers. I'd like to try it on."

The saleslady got the hat out of the window and Timmie was more sure than ever that it was a lampshade. But then the saleslady perched it on Mother's head, and it didn't look like a lampshade at all any more. It looked like the most beautiful hat Timmie had ever seen.

"Oh!" he said, "it's beautiful!"

"Do you like it, Timmie?" Mother asked.

"Yes," Timmie said. "Why don't you buy it?"

But Mother wasn't quite sure, then. "You don't think it looks like a lampshade, do you?"

"No," Timmie said, "I think it looks like a hat. And I think it's just beautiful. And I think you ought to buy it."

But Mother still wasn't quite sure. "You don't think it's silly, do you?" she asked.

"No," Timmie said. "I think it's just beautiful."

So Mother said she'd think about it, and then she and Timmie went out of the store and started down the Boulevard again.

They hadn't gone very far when they saw a woman wearing a hat just like the one Mother had tried on.

"Look!" Mother said. "There's *my* hat!"

"Look!" Timmie said. "There's Isabelle!"

He ran after her. "Bonjour," he said.

Isabelle was holding the hand of the lady wearing the hat like the one Mother tried on. When Timmie spoke to her, she dropped the lady's hand and turned around. "Bonjour," she said and grinned. Then she said something to the lady that Timmie couldn't understand.

Just then Mother hurried up. Mother said "Bonjour" to the woman, too, and then they shook hands, just the way Timmie and the little girl did.

After Mother talked to the woman for what seemed a long time, because Timmie could hardly understand anything she said, she turned around to him. "This is Isabelle's mother," she said. "And she says that she and Isabelle are going to market. Would you like to go with them?"

"Yes," Timmie said. "Of course I would."

So Mother kissed Timmie on both cheeks, just the way the French do when you're quite grown-up, and off Timmie went with Isabelle and her mother, swinging Isabelle's hand as they strode along.

But they didn't go to the market right away.

First they went to the apartment where Isabelle lived. And Isabelle's mother took off her hat (it was much too beautiful to wear to market) but she didn't take off her gloves. Everyone in Paris, Timmie noticed, even little boys like him and little girls like Isabelle, wore gloves.

Then Isabelle's mother gave Timmie a big straw basket to carry and she gave Isabelle a little sack

made of string which she called a "fi-let" (*fee-leh*). She took another basket for herself and *then* they started off.

They went through some little narrow streets that wound around and twisted and turned and were so tiny that Timmie was sure he could touch the buildings on both sides if he stretched his arms out wide.

They stopped to stare into the windows of the sort of shops that Timmie could hardly have dreamed of—one with swords and suits of armor big enough to wear, another filled as full as full could be with soldiers no bigger than Timmie's tiny finger, and still another with stuffed owls and squirrels and monkeys and a great big dog that made Timmie just a tiny bit homesick, because it looked so much like Rover, back in America.

But they didn't stop for long.

They went on until they came to a very wide street, with the big trees Mother said were chestnut trees lining both sides.

And there, right in the middle of the street, and just as far as Timmie could see, were little stands exactly like the ones at the County Fair.

But these stands were piled high with vegetables and fruits, and meats.

There were great mounds of rich, ripe, rosy tomatoes, and mountains of cauliflowers and cabbages and crispy carrots that were the color of the sun when Timmie looked at it with his eyes closed.

There were heaps of skinny string beans, and radishes like rubies, and lettuce the color of emeralds.

And there were artichokes that looked like gray-green water lilies about to burst into bloom.

There were peaches and plums and apricots and cherries that glistened red in the sun.

And there were berries.

Raspberries in boxes and strawberries in bins and little baby berries that Isabelle called "fraises des bois" (*frez deh bwah*) in little baby baskets.

They walked along between the rows of stands and Isabelle's mother bought potatoes and tomatoes

and onions and carrots and celery and then a plump, pink chicken and a dozen eggs and a great round, red cheese, and a little white one, and she put them all in Timmie's basket.

When Timmie's basket was full and Isabelle's shopping bag was stuffed with oranges and bananas and peaches and cherries, they all crossed the street to a shop with a sign that said "Boulangerie" (*boo-lahnz-ree*) and Isabelle's mother bought long loaves of bread, as tall as Timmie, to take home, and chocolate-covered cakes to eat right then.

Timmie was sure their shopping was over. But when they came out of the bakery, Isabelle's mother led Timmie and Isabelle on, down between the rows of booths, to where people were selling flowers.

They had stopped in front of a stand that was covered with red carnations and blue bachelor's-buttons and yellow roses when Timmie felt a tug at his basket.

At first he thought it was just because the basket was so heavy and he shifted his hand a little.

But then he felt the tug again (it was almost like the time he had caught the fish) and he turned to look.

And there, standing right beside him, was a little gray donkey with big, pointed ears, and, on both sides of his back, baskets filled with sweet-smelling lavender.

And the little donkey had his head down and his nose in Timmie's basket, and he was nonchalantly nibbling the bright green tops of the carrots.

"He's hungry!" Timmie said. "The poor little thing!" And then Isabelle's mother turned around and saw what was happening and she gave Timmie and Isabelle carrots to feed to the donkey.

He snapped at the carrots greedily—not politely at all—and Timmie wanted to give him another and another and another. Timmie wanted to give the

donkey *all* the carrots. But he knew Isabelle's mother wouldn't have anything left for dinner if he did. So he just patted the donkey's head and the donkey nuzzled Timmie's cheek with his soft, cold nose.

And then it was time to go.

But before they left, Timmie bought a packet of the sweet-smelling lavender to take home to Mother.

Timmie and Isabelle and Isabelle's mother went back through the narrow, winding streets with their heavy baskets and their flowers and their loaves of bread.

They didn't windowshop this time.

They just went straight home.

Timmie hurried into the hotel because he wanted to tell Mother all about the little donkey and the market and the shops. And there, waiting for the elevator, was Mother.

She was wearing the big, round, white beautiful hat with the feathers on it.

"Oh!" Timmie said, "but it's beautiful!" And then he gave Mother the packet of sweet-smelling lavender.

"Timmie, darling!" Mother said. She put her arms around him and gave him a hug and a kiss. "Thank you."

Timmie pointed to the hat. "It's beautiful!" he said again.

And Mother said, "Paris is a woman's town."

Timmie thought it was just the place for little boys.

4

The Eiffel Tower

Timmie knew it was going to be a wonderful day as soon as he woke up. It was going to be a happy, exciting day.

He could just feel that it was.

Even before he was out of bed, while his head was still deep in his soft and fluffy pillow, and he was still watching the sunbeams dancing in and out around the brass columns of the bed, Mother opened the door, poked her head in to see if he was awake, and said, "Timmie, dear, it's a wonderful day!"

Timmie sat straight up.

"Oh, yes," he said, "it's a wonderful day. Mother, let's do something special today. It's such a *wonderful* day!"

Mother came in and sat down on the edge of Timmie's bed.

"Yes," she said. "Let's."

"But what?" Timmie asked. "What shall we do?"

Mother knew right away what to do on such a day. "We'll go to the Eiffel Tower," she said.

Timmie hopped out of bed. "Yes," he said. "Let's."

Timmie started to look for his shoes. "Mother," he said, when he found the left one, "can we take Isabelle with us?"

"Of course," Mother said. She fished Timmie's right shoe out from under the radiator. "I'll go and call her, now."

Timmie got dressed as fast as a fireman when he hears the alarm. He reached the breakfast table even before Mother and Daddy did. And he was all ready, with his face washed and his hair combed and neatly parted, when Isabelle knocked at the door.

The four of them squeezed into a tiny taxi that went zooming down the boulevards and zipping around corners and racing through the narrow streets, which is the way taxis always go in Paris.

Long before they reached the Eiffel Tower, Timmie could see it. From quite far off it looked just like a tower that he might have built himself, with his Erector set.

But the tower grew larger and larger as Timmie and Mother and Daddy and Isabelle got nearer and nearer and nearer.

When they finally reached it, Timmie could see that the Eiffel Tower wasn't a toy at all. It was almost as high as some of the buildings in New York. Still, it was different. It wasn't made of brick or concrete or stone, but of great steel girders bolted together.

To Timmie it still looked as if it had been built with an Erector set, but, of course, the most enormous one in all the world.

They walked over to a door marked "Entrée" (*awn-treh*) and got in line for the elevator. It was a very long line and Timmie was impatient. He didn't want to wait.

He wanted to race up the stairs.

But Mother shook her head and laughed and said, "Oh, no, Timmie. I'm too old to climb all those steps."

When the elevator came at last, everybody—
Timmie and Isabelle and Mother and Daddy and
little girls with their daddies and little boys with
their mothers, and people who were tourists and
spoke all different languages, and American soldiers
and sailors and Marines—all pushed and shoved
and crowded their way inside.

The elevator was more like a streetcar than any
elevator Timmie had ever seen. It had big windows
on three sides and a bench at the back.

And when it started it went very fast and it tipped
forward. Timmie pressed his face against the glass
and below him he could see the green grass of the
park, going farther and farther away, and above
him he could see the blue of the Paris sky, getting

nearer and nearer, and between the beams of the Tower, he could see the buildings of Paris.

When they reached the first landing, a lot of people pushed and shoved and crowded their way out, and a lot more pushed and shoved and crowded their way in.

And when they reached the second landing, everybody got out, and Mother and Daddy and Timmie and Isabelle got into another elevator because *they* were going all the way to the top.

When they finally reached the top, Timmie darted out of the elevator and rushed over to the railing. There below him, and all around, was Paris.

It looked like a little village under the Christmas tree, and the buildings looked like wooden blocks, and the trees seemed to be balls of green cotton growing on wooden pegs and the flower beds here and there were like bright-colored beads.

And everything made a pattern.

Right under the Tower was a long, narrow park, like a big, wide street of green grass. At one end of the park was the Military College that was low and long and grimy-gray. Daddy told Timmie that the park was called the "Champ-de-Mars" (*shawng-duh-mahrss*) and that once upon a time, long, long

ago, the cadets from the Military College had paraded there.

At the other end of the Champ-de-Mars was a sparkling clean, white building that was very new. It was the Palais de Chaillot (*pa-leh duh shie-yoh*). When Timmie asked about it, Daddy said it wasn't the kind of palace that people lived in ever, but was a place with theaters and museums and exhibition halls, and that it even had an aquarium, with strange and rare fish swimming about.

Daddy showed Timmie and Isabelle the Grand (*grawng*) Palais, (he told Timmie that "grand" meant "large") across the Seine (*sen*), with a huge, rounded roof, and near it the Petit (*puh-tee*) (which meant "little") Palais, with a smaller, rounded roof.

After that they walked all around the platform, way up there near the top of the Tower. Mother pointed out a cathedral with two square towers, just alike, that was Notre Dame (*nohtr dahm*), and then Daddy showed them all a great big church, on

the highest hill in Paris. "That's Sacré Coeur" (*sack-ray kerr*), he said. Sacré Coeur had fat round towers, like turnips turned upside down, and it was white and shiny in the sunlight.

All over Paris, Timmie could see tall, slender spires of churches. And there were lots of big, fat domes, too. One of them was even made of gold, and Mother told Timmie that was Les Invalides (*lehz ahn-vah-leed*), where the Emperor Napoleon was buried. Then she showed him another dome, the Panthéon (*pawn-tay-ong*), that held the tombs of other great men of France.

Daddy showed Timmie the Arc de Triomphe (*ark duh tree-awmf*). It was set in the middle of broad avenues, all lined with trees. The avenues formed a star, and Daddy said the circle where the arch stood was called "l'Etoile" (*leh-twahl*), the French word for "star."

Winding in and out around all the buildings Timmie could see was a thin thread of blue. It was the River Seine. There were so many bridges across the river that Timmie couldn't even count them.

He was still trying, though, when Isabelle discovered the telescopes in one corner. Daddy gave them each a one-franc piece and they dropped the money in the slots. When they peered through the telescopes they could see everything that was really far off brought right up close. Timmie could even see the Bois de Boulogne (*bwah duh boo-low-nyeh*), on the very edge of Paris, with its lakes, one after another in a chain, and he was quite sure he saw people rowing on one of the lakes.

They walked all around the platform once more, and they stopped on the side where the Seine grows wide and spreads off into the hills and flows on to the sea.

Then Daddy said, "Before we go, Timmie, I think you and Isabelle ought to have your pictures taken."

Timmie thought so, too, but he didn't see Daddy's camera. "Where?" he asked.

"Over there," Daddy said. He pointed to a little shop right behind them. So they all went over and Timmie and Isabelle stood behind a screen that had a drawing of the Eiffel Tower on the front of it, and they stuck their heads through a hole near the top. The Tower in the drawing was very small, and their heads were very large, and they both looked so funny

that everybody laughed. And that was when the photographer snapped the picture.

After they'd had their pictures taken, Mother said, "I think we ought to go, Timmie. It's almost time for lunch."

But Timmie didn't want to go, and Daddy didn't, either. So Daddy said, "Let's all have lunch here!"

They went down to a big restaurant with velvet-covered benches and clean white tablecloths, and shining glasses and sparkling silver, and the waiter took them right over to a table next to a huge window.

While they ate, Timmie watched the cars, no bigger than the ones Santa left in his Christmas stocking, going back and forth over the bridges.

After lunch, Timmie and Isabelle walked all around the Tower one more time.

Then they ran all the way down the curling, round-about stairway . . . not because they were in a hurry, but just because it was such fun to see the sky above and the earth below and the buildings of Paris all flash by.

Mother and Daddy followed them down the stairs, too, but much more slowly. Mother wasn't too old, she said, to walk *down*. Still, she couldn't keep up with Timmie.

And just as soon as they reached home, Timmie got his blocks and his Tinker Toys and his construction sets out of the toy chest. He and Isabelle built a tower just like the Eiffel Tower right square in the center of the rug in Timmie's room.

It wasn't a very tall tower, but Timmie pretended it was.

He pretended, too, that he could see all of Paris from it.

5

Les Invalides

Timmie and Isabelle and Mother and Daddy were all going to Les Invalides. "We'll see the Tomb of Napoleon, first," Mother said. "And then we'll go to the Museum of the Army. I think you'll like it."

Daddy was just going to call a taxi when Timmie spotted an old-fashioned carriage drawn by a horse and driven by a red-faced man wearing a black bowler hat. "Look!" Timmie said, pointing.

"Shall we go in that, Tim?" Daddy asked.

Timmie was so thrilled at the thought of going in the carriage that he couldn't even say "yes." He could only nod his head.

But Daddy understood, so they all piled in and the driver whirled his whip in a great circle and cracked it in the air and off they went.

On the way to Les Invalides, Daddy told Timmie about Napoleon. "He was the Emperor of France," Daddy said. Timmie wanted to know what an emperor was.

"It's like a king," Daddy told him. "Only more important, because he ruled many countries. Napoleon was a great general, and he led the French armies to victory over Italy and Austria and Spain."

Napoléon
1769 — 1821

"When?" Timmie asked. "Was it a long time ago?"

"Yes," Daddy said. "He was born almost two hundred years ago."

"And what happened to him?"

"Well, he was defeated by the British, in a famous battle called 'The Battle of Waterloo.' After that, he had to leave France. He died on a tiny island, St. Helena, nearly a hundred and fifty years ago. But he did many things for the people of France. He built schools and roads and bridges, and made good laws, and he helped the people to become rich. That's why he's still considered the greatest French hero, and that's why he's buried here!" The carriage had stopped and Daddy pointed to the building in front of them. It was the one with the golden dome Timmie had seen from the Eiffel Tower.

The building was dark and dirty on the outside, but when they stepped through the door, Timmie saw that it was all white marble with golden eagles and golden angels all around, like a fairyland. It was very large, and very, very high, and in the dome in the center were beautiful paintings in blue and gold.

The building was dimly lit, with light coming through the blue glass windows that were all around it, except at one end where the window was of gold.

It was hushed and quiet and everybody spoke in whispers, the way they always do in church.

In the very center of the room, and way below where Timmie and Isabelle stood, was a great red and green granite monument.

It was Napoleon's Tomb.

Timmie thought Napoleon must have been a very big man, to have such a big tomb. But Daddy said no, he wasn't very much taller than Timmie.

Timmie and Isabelle and Mother and Daddy walked all the way around the railing above the tomb, and then they went downstairs and through the great bronze doors that had laurel leaves carved on them and through other doors that were painted gold and had eagles, too.

Then a guide came, and they all walked around the tomb again, while the guide told them all about Napoleon, and showed them the statues in honor of his greatest victories. And when they came to a glass case with Napoleon's hat and the medals on wide green and yellow ribbons, the guide let down a velvet rope so that Timmie and Isabelle could go right up close to the case and look at them.

Then the guide led them back to the golden doors and said "Bonjour" very politely to Mother and

Daddy. But he winked at Timmie and patted Isabelle's head.

Timmie and Isabelle tiptoed up the stairs and out of the building because they knew they should be very quiet in Les Invalides.

Outside, the sun was very bright. Timmie blinked and then he saw a sign that said "Musée de l'Armée" (*mew-zay duh larm-ay*). He ran around the corner with Isabelle following him. When Mother and Daddy caught up with them, they went through a door and down a long corridor and through another door.

Timmie blinked again and looked around.

They were on a terrace, with a large courtyard in the middle. And hanging from the walls of the building and propped against it and leaning on pillars

77

were cannons. Big cannons and little cannons and very old ones and new ones, too. And scattered through the cobbled courtyard were even bigger cannons.

Timmie wanted to examine every one, but Daddy led them through a plain wooden door, and into one of the buildings around the court.

Timmie blinked a third time.

He was in the middle of a hall as big as a hotel lobby, and twice as big as the schoolroom back home. And it was filled, from one end to the other, with suits of armor.

There were striped suits of armor, and checked and patterned and plain. There was armor with stripes going up and down, and with stripes going around, and with stripes slanted this way and that.

There was armor for men and armor for horses and even armor for little boys just Timmie's size.

And there were gleaming silver swords and shining shields and helmets. And great gold saddles for horses, and silver ones, too, and ones of red and blue velvet that kings had ridden on.

Timmie roamed from one to another, stopping and staring, and wishing all the time that he had lived in the days when people really wore the things he saw.

And long before Timmie grew tired of looking at the armor, Mother said, "I think we'd better go on to the next building."

When Timmie went into the next great hall, he forgot all about the armor, because this one was full of flags.

There were cases of flags and flags over the cases
and rows of flags over *those* flags and still more flags
hanging from the ceiling.

There were old flags with gold emblems and
golden flags and green flags and blue, white, and red
French flags. There were battle flags and regimental
flags and flags of the cavalry units and flags of the
infantry.

Some of the flags were torn and tattered and half
shot away. There were rags of flags and scraps
of flags and shreds of flags that had crumbled with
age.

And then there were pictures on the wall of the
great battles Napoleon had fought, and, in a
case against the wall, Timmie saw Napoleon's over-
coat and his uniform.

In another building, Timmie saw rows and rows of uniforms—red and blue, and white ones for the desert, and tall hats with plumes and hats made of fur and hats with tassels.

And he saw cases of medals and other cases of muskets and pistols, and still others filled with coins.

In a tiny room upstairs, Timmie saw the very bed that Napoleon had slept on. And farther on he saw the desk and books and chairs that had belonged to General Lafayette, who had fought in the American Revolution.

Timmie wasn't nearly ready to go when the bell rang at closing time. *He* could have stayed forever.

And even though Mother and Daddy hurried him along, Timmie was the last one to leave before the guards locked the doors for the night.

On the way home, Timmie said to Mother, "Do you know what I'm going to be when I grow up?"

Mother looked at the policeman who was holding up his white stick to stop traffic. "A policeman?" she guessed.

"No," Timmie said.

Just then a fire truck came around the corner, filled with pompiers (*pohm-pee-ay*) in shiny steel helmets. "A fireman?" Daddy asked.

"No."

Mother looked up in the air. There was a big silver airplane on its way to New York. "I know," she said. "An airplane pilot."

"No," Timmie said. "I'm going to be a general."

6

Along the Seine

Timmie was thinking very hard. He sat at the big
desk in the hotel room and chewed the end of his
pencil and sometimes he put the tip of it in his
mouth, and then he wrinkled up his forehead and
thought.

Timmie was writing a letter.

It was a letter to his grandmother, back in America,
and Timmie was telling her all about Paris.

"Dear Grandma," he wrote, "I hope you are feeling well. I am. Paris is very . . ." and then he stopped.

"Mother," he called.

Mother looked up from the letter *she* was writing. "Yes, Timmie?" she said.

"How do you spell 'beautiful'?" Timmie asked.

"B-e-a-u . . ." Mother spelled. Timmie wrote it down carefully.

". . . Paris is very beautiful."

Then he stopped and chewed on his pencil again. "How do you spell 'specially'?"

Mother spelled that for him, too.

"I specially like the Luxembourg Gardens," he scribbled. He read over what he had written.

"Mother," he asked, "what do you specially like in Paris?"

Mother knew at once. "The shops," she said. "The little shops with the lovely clothes."

Timmie looked over at Daddy who was sitting in the big brown armchair, reading a newspaper. "What do *you* like, specially, in Paris?" he asked.

Daddy looked at Timmie over the top of the paper. "Me?" he asked. "I think I like to wander along the Seine."

"The Seine?" Timmie said.

"That's the river. You know, the one we could see from the Eiffel Tower," Mother said.

"But I've never walked along it," Timmie said.

Daddy put his paper down. He looked out the win-

dow and Timmie did, too, and they could both see that the sun was shining, and the sky was the light clear blue of spring. "It's a perfect day for a walk," Daddy said. "Are you ready, Tim?"

"Yes," Timmie said. Timmie was *always* ready to go walking with Daddy. "Let's see if we can find Isabelle. She might like to go, too."

Then Daddy said to Mother, "Let's all go!"

So Mother finished her letter and Timmie found Isabelle and Daddy put more film in his camera.

When everybody was ready, Daddy said, "We'll take the bus to the Pont Neuf (*pohng nuhf*) and walk across it and up the Right Bank."

Timmie wanted to know what the "Pont Neuf" was.

"It's a bridge," Daddy said. "'Pont Neuf' means 'New Bridge'."

"Is it new?" Timmie asked.

Daddy laughed. "No," he said. "It's the oldest bridge in Paris. But that's what it's called. 'Pont Neuf'."

Timmie thought that was sillier than anything he'd yet heard. But on the bus, on the way to the bridge, when Timmie and Daddy were standing on the back platform the way Timmie had always wanted to, Daddy explained that years and years ago—over three hundred and fifty years ago—when the bridge was built, all the people of Paris liked to walk across it and to see the Fair that was always held there and to watch jugglers and acrobats who performed near it. They'd called it the 'New Bridge' then, and even when newer ones were built, they kept on calling it that.

When Daddy and Mother and Timmie and Isabelle reached the bridge, they got off the bus and started to walk across, just the way Parisians have for so long. But long before they got to the little island that divides it in two—Daddy called it "La Cité" (*lah see-tay*)—they stopped to lean over the railing.

There were boats on the river; flat-bottomed boats

carrying oil and other flat-bottomed boats carrying coal, and Timmie even saw a flat-bottomed houseboat, where people lived, with a little dog scurrying around the deck. Then a big white boat came sailing majestically up the Seine, and passed under the bridge. It was hung from stem to stern with gaily colored flags, and the decks were crowded with people dressed in bright, light clothes, and there were yellow and purple chairs and orange and green umbrellas.

"What's that?" Timmie asked.

"It's a sightseeing boat," Daddy said. "It's called a 'bateau mouche' (*bah-toh moosh*). It goes up the river, from one end of Paris to the other. And people can see all the city from the Seine."

They watched the bateau mouche until it disap-

peared behind the second little island, the Ile St-Louis (*eel san lwee*). Then Timmie saw that there were still other boats, like little rowboats, anchored along the banks of the river. And standing or sitting, or sometimes lying down, all along the banks, were fishermen with long poles. They never seemed to move, except to pull their lines out of the water.

But they weren't catching any fish!

Daddy said they almost *never* caught any fish!

Timmie and Isabelle hung over the railing, looking down into the water. And while they were both looking, Daddy snapped their pictures.

Then Daddy said, "We'd better go on, Tim. There's lots more to see."

So Timmie and Isabelle climbed down off the railing and trotted along after Mother and Daddy.

They had almost reached the Ile de la Cité when Timmie, who was looking down and being very careful not to step on the cracks in the pavement, heard Mother say, "Careful, Timmie."

He looked up right away. And there, standing on the bridge, was a man with a beret on his head and a paint brush in his hand. He was standing behind an easel and looking off at the cathedral on the island (it was Notre Dame), while he worked.

Timmie darted around behind him and peered over his shoulder at the picture the man was painting.

It didn't look like Notre Dame at all—or hardly like it! The picture was all squares and circles and blocks! But Timmie was sure it would be a very beautiful picture and when the man turned around he said, very politely, "It's very beautiful, Monsieur" (*muss-yah*).

Then Timmie ran off and took Daddy's hand. And he didn't even smile until they had reached the other side of the Seine.

Timmie was going to ask Mother about the painting, but he didn't have a chance to, because they crossed the street and Timmie heard squeaking and squawking and squealing almost like Isabelle's school, but when he looked around for children, he didn't see any.

What he saw was a shop with rows and rows of cages in front. And in the cages were chickens and baby ducks and rabbits and pigeons and white doves and yellow canaries and green parrots and blue lovebirds and tiny red and brown birds and other tiny birds that seemed to be all colors of the rainbow and a lot of colors, too, that weren't even in the rainbow.

Timmie looked up the Quai (*kay*).

All along it were shops like this one, with cages and tanks and bowls and boxes out in front. Timmie and Isabelle strolled from one to the other, stopping to look at tiny white mice with pink ears and long pink tails scampering back and forth in glass tanks.

They saw cages with squirrels and boxes with turtles and bowls with goldfish, and sometimes little plastic bags with goldfish in them, too, and once, a big aquarium with writhing, wriggling snakes that Mother and Isabelle didn't want to look at.

Then they saw little baskets with puppies and kittens that Isabelle wanted so much to look at that she stopped right in front of them. "Ooh!" she sighed. "Ils sont mignons" (*eel zont meen-yon*).

Timmie, too, thought they were the cutest puppies and kittens he had ever seen. So they walked along,

hand in hand, stopping in front of every single pet shop. And when they reached the very last one, Timmie asked Isabelle what she liked best.

Isabelle pointed to a fluffy, furry, white kitten that would just fit into her two hands. "J'aime le joli chat" (*zhem luh zhoh-lee shah*), she said.

"And what do you like, Tim?" Daddy asked.

"I like the white mice," Timmie declared. "Can I buy some? Please, Daddy."

But before Daddy could say "yes," Mother said, "Oh, no, Timmie. *Not* white mice!"

"Turtles?" Timmie asked hopefully.

Mother shook her head.

Timmie thought a big, black snake would be nice, too, but he was sure Mother wouldn't like that any more than white mice.

Then Timmie turned around and he forgot all about snakes and turtles and mice. Because just across the bridge was a great enormous castle, with sloping roofs and tiny windows and pointed towers.

Timmie was sure that kings and queens and even little princes must have lived in it, once, and Daddy said that was exactly right. The earliest kings of France had lived in that very place.

Just then a man came by, pushing a little cart that was loaded with flowers. Timmie went up to Daddy and whispered in his ear.

"Not now," Daddy whispered back. "We'll go to the Flower Market."

And then they turned a corner and Timmie closed his eyes and took a deep breath and something smelled sweet and spicy at the same time, like the way Mother's room had smelled when Timmie had spilled her perfume.

And when Timmie opened his eyes, he saw flowers all around him. Purple violets and red roses and pink carnations and bunches of red and blue anemones and yellow and lavender and crimson gladioli and pots of green ferns with shiny leaves and fragile white lilies of the valley.

Timmie ran after Daddy and tugged on his hand,

and Daddy said, "Yes, Timmie. We'll buy some
flowers for Mother here." So they bought a big
bouquet of yellow roses for Timmie's mother, and
pink carnations for Isabelle's mother. And for Isabelle, they bought a little bunch of lilies of the valley
—muguet des bois (*mew-gay day bwah*).

Isabelle was so delighted that she clapped her
hands. "Ca porte bonheur!" (*saw port bohn-uhr*) she
said, telling Timmie that lilies of the valley, just like

four-leaf clovers back home, were supposed to bring good luck.

When they reached the end of the Flower Market, Daddy asked, "Tired, Tim?"

Timmie shook his head and when Daddy looked at Isabelle, she shook hers, too.

So they all walked over to Notre Dame.

The little park in front of it was filled with pigeons that swirled around in the air and dived and strutted along the paths. Daddy bought a little bag of seed from a vendor who stood in front of the gates of the Cathedral, and Timmie and Isabelle sprinkled them on the ground for the pigeons and then they put some in their hands and the pigeons came and settled on their shoulders and arms and wrists and pecked at the seeds they held out.

After the pigeons had eaten all the seeds and flown off, without even saying "Thank you," Daddy looked at his watch and said, "I think we'd better go."

So they crossed another bridge, a very small one, this time, and walked down the Left Bank of the Seine. On one side of the street, right along the river, there was an unbroken row of green-painted book-stalls.

But Timmie and Isabelle wanted to walk on the other side, where they could look in shop windows.

They had stopped in front of one that was full of pictures of sailing ships when Daddy said, "This is 'The Street of the Fishing Cat'."

It was the tiniest street that Timmie had ever seen.

It was so tiny, he wouldn't have known it was a street at all if Daddy hadn't told him.

It wasn't any bigger than the driveway that led to the garage at home.

But there on the wall of a building was a blue and white street sign that said "Rue du Chat-qui-Pêche" (*rew doo shah kee pehsh*) "The Street of the Fishing Cat."

Timmie ran all the way to the end and back. It just took him half a minute because the street was so short. But when he came back, Daddy said, "You surely must be tired now, Tim. Let's take a taxi."

They all went to a café (*caffay*) near the hotel, and they all sat out in the open air, under a striped awning, and Mother and Daddy ordered black coffee —café noir (*caffay nwahr*)—and Timmie and Isabelle drank soda.

And when a man with a little black, pointed beard came into the café, Timmie thought at first that it was Abraham Lincoln. But Daddy laughed and said, "That's just another artist, Tim."

They were almost ready to leave when Daddy said, "What are you thinking about, Tim?"

"I'm thinking that I don't want to be a general, after all," Timmie said. "I want to be a painter and wear a beard. And I'm going to live," he added, "on 'The Street of the Fishing Cat'."

7

Up the Hill . . .

Isabelle was teaching Timmie to count.

"Un (*uhng*) . . . deux (*duh*) . . . trois (*trwah*) . . ." she said in French. And after Timmie repeated the French words, he said, so that Isabelle could learn English, "One . . . two . . . three."

"Quatre (*kahtr*) . . . cinq (*sank*) . . . six (*seess*) . . ." Isabelle went on.

"Quatre . . . cinq . . . six . . ." Timmie repeated after her. "Four . . . five . . . six."

"Sept (*set*) . . . huit (*weet*) . . . neuf (*nuff*) . . . dix (*deess*)."

"Sept . . . huit . . . neuf . . . dix," Timmie said. "Seven . . . eight . . . nine . . . ten."

That reminded him of something. "Seven . . . eight . . . nine . . ." What was it? Seven . . . eight . . . and then Timmie remembered.

In eight days, Timmie and Mother and Daddy were going to leave Paris.

Timmie was quite sure of it. But he wanted to be surer, still. He rushed into the room where Mother was making a list of all the gifts she was planning to take back with her.

"Mother," Timmie said, "when are we going back home?"

Mother looked up at Timmie and smiled. "In eight days," she said.

"Oh!" Timmie couldn't help sounding disappointed.

"What's the matter, Tim?" Daddy asked.

"I don't want to go home," Timmie said.

"Don't you want to see Betty again?" Mother asked. "And Joey and Laura?"

"Well . . . yes . . ." Timmie said.

"And Rover?" Daddy asked.

"Yes," Timmie said. "Yes, I do. But I don't want to leave Paris."

"I can't blame you, Tim," Daddy said. "Maybe we can come back, though."

"When?"

Daddy wasn't sure. "Sometime," he said.

"But I want to see all of Paris before I go," Timmie said. "And all at once."

"Well . . ." Daddy thought for a minute, ". . . well, Tim," he said, "if you want to see all of Paris all at once, it seems to me the place to go is Montmartre" (*mohn-mahrtr*).

So that's where they went. All of them. Mother and Daddy and Isabelle and Timmie.

And because it was so much quicker, they went by the Métropolitan (*meh-troh-pohl-ee-tan*), which Daddy called the "Métro" (*meh-troh*) for short. Timmie learned even without asking that the Métro was a subway—a whole long train that went underground.

Daddy bought tickets and Timmie handed them to the man at the gate. Then they all walked down the long platform and when the train came, they got into the middle car.

They whizzed through a long, dark tunnel, from

103

one white tiled station to another. And in almost no time, they had reached their station.

When Timmie and Isabelle and Mother and Daddy came out of the subway, they were at the bottom of a very steep hill. "We'll take the finicular from here," Daddy said.

The "finicular" turned out to be a little trolley-like car that went up almost to the top of the hill. It was sort of like the subway, Timmie thought, only smaller. And sort of like the elevator at the Eiffel Tower, too, only bigger.

It went part way up and then Timmie and Isabelle and Mother and Daddy got out and Timmie saw they were standing in front of a long, long row of steps. And at the very top of the steps was the Sacré-Coeur—the church with the white turrets Mother had pointed out before.

They all started up the steps and Timmie and Isabelle counted as they climbed. "Un . . . deux . . . trois . . . quatre . . ."

But Timmie could only count to ten in French and there were so many steps Timmie wasn't even sure he could count that high in English. So, after he had counted to ten three times, he and Isabelle both stopped counting and ran up the rest of the steps together.

At the top of the stairs, they stopped to wait for Mother and Daddy.

Below them, just as at the Eiffel Tower, was Paris.

And Daddy had been right.

There was all of Paris.

Timmie could see the golden dome of Les Invalides. Over there, rising high above the rest of Paris, was the Eiffel Tower. There was the Panthéon, and there was Notre Dame, and there was the spire of Sainte-Chapelle (*sant shap-ell*).

Timmie and Isabelle didn't say a word. They looked at Paris for a long time.

They looked at Paris until Daddy said, "We ought to see Montmartre, too, Tim."

So they turned away from all the places Timmie knew and went up more stairs and turned into a narrow, curving road. The street was cobbled and uneven, and the sidewalks, too, were tiny and very rough. Timmie had to walk very slowly to keep from tripping on the stones.

The buildings along the way were very old and most of them were very small, and they were painted different colors—yellow and pink and red and green. They tipped and tilted and leaned on one

another, as though they were too old to stand up straight all by themselves.

Timmie noticed that most of them had red-and-white or blue-and-white or green-and-white checked curtains at the windows. Some of the buildings were houses and some of them were restaurants and others were cafés. And there were lots of tiny shops, too, and Timmie saw that most of those sold pictures.

He found out why when they reached the Place du Tertre (*plahs doo tair-tre*). There, in a little square no bigger than Timmie's backyard at home, were dozens and dozens of tables crowded together, with bright striped umbrellas shading them from the

sun. And all around the Place were artists, like the one Timmie had seen on the Pont Neuf. They all had easels and they all wore berets and they were all painting pictures of the Place du Tertre and of Sacré-Coeur and of the people wandering around.

Timmie and Isabelle wanted to have their pictures painted, too, but Daddy looked at his watch and said, "We haven't time, Tim."

"Why?" Timmie wanted to know.

"You'll see," Daddy said, and he winked at Mother, and she winked back, and then they both smiled at Timmie and Isabelle.

But they wouldn't tell Timmie why.

And Timmie didn't find out, until they had walked down the hill to one of the most crowded streets of Paris, where people were bustling back and forth in a great hurry—not at all the way they'd wandered around Montmartre.

They stopped in front of a squat, round-domed building, and at first Timmie thought it was a theater.

And then he saw posters all around.

"It's a circus!" Timmie shouted.

"It's a circus," Daddy said. He led them all inside, and gave the tickets to an usher who took

them to the very first row and pointed out four seats right next to the railing.

Timmie clambered onto his seat and looked around him.

This was a circus—Daddy had said so, and he'd seen the posters—but it wasn't like any circus Timmie had ever seen.

It was more like a tiny theater, with a little round stage in the center of the building. That was the ring, and it wasn't even covered with sawdust, but with a coarse brown mat.

Timmie had never seen a circus before that wasn't in a tent. But this was a special building just for the circus, and Daddy said it was open all year round. Still, the building *looked* like a tent, with painted flowers strewn across the top of it.

Les Eléphants!

Le Léopard en équilibre!

L'ours patinant!

All around the wall were circus pictures. There were gypsies and acrobats and clowns and elephants on barrels and dogs jumping through hoops and sword swallowers and dancing bears, too.

Timmie turned all the way around, to see *all* the pictures, and he'd just settled back in his seat when Daddy said, "Let's go see the animals."

So he and Timmie and Isabelle trooped out, beyond the lobby. And they found three tiny elephants —well, for *elephants* they were tiny—and seven spotted leopards in a cage and a little gray donkey eating hay. Daddy said they would all be in the circus.

Just as the band started to play, they hurried back to their seats.

All the lights went out and then other lights over the center of the ring went on. A whole band

of clowns came rolling and reeling and tumbling across the ring. Their faces were painted white and they had pointed caps on their heads and satin suits with baggy pants and they all turned somersaults and cartwheels and handsprings.

And when all those clowns had run around the ring three times, pushing each other and falling down and getting up again and tripping over their own feet (that were at least twice as big as any feet Timmie had ever seen), another clown came skipping into the ring.

His name was Boum Boum and he sang a song that made everyone laugh and then he danced and walked and whirled and pranced from one side of the ring to the other.

And then he waltzed right over to where Timmie was sitting *and shook his hand!*

After Boum Boum had run off, Timmie and Isabelle and Mother and Daddy watched acrobats in spangled tights who climbed to the tiptop of tall poles and hung from them, twirling about by one foot or one finger.

They watched jugglers who kept balls and clubs and rings spinning high in the air.

They watched horses jump through hoops and then they watched the little elephants dance, posing on one foot on pedestals, swinging their trunks.

While the band played, the ring was turned into a huge cage, and seven spotted leopards came leaping into it and climbed up on high stools.

Then a man wearing a leopard skin, just like Tarzan, walked fearlessly into the cage. The leopards growled and snarled and roared, but they couldn't frighten the man. He shook a short stick at them, and they jumped through hoops, too, and walked across tightropes and climbed high ladders.

While the band played again, the cage was dismantled and the little donkey came out and carted it off.

Then everyone came back—the clowns and the acrobats and the jugglers and the horses and the elephants and the man who trained the leopards, (but of course, *not* the leopards)—all came back and marched around the ring three times, and everyone in the audience applauded very loud and very long and the circus was over.

Everybody got up to leave.

Timmie and Isabelle struggled into their coats and started out with Mother and Daddy.

People were pushing each other, crowded close together, swarming to the doors.

Isabelle slipped her hand into one of Mother's. Daddy held out his hand for Timmie's.

But Timmie shoved his hand deep into his pocket.

It was the hand that Boum Boum had shaken.

8

. . . and Back

Everybody got up early.

Timmie was up before the sun rose, and Mother was up before Timmie, and Daddy was up even before Mother.

And everybody was hurrying back and forth, packing the last suitcase and saying "Have we forgotten anything?" and looking out the window to say "Good-by" to Paris.

And then, much too soon, everything was ready and Timmie and Mother and Daddy were eating croissants and butter curls and strawberry jam and drinking hot chocolate and café au lait for the last time.

And breakfast—Timmie had learned to call it "petit déjeuner" (*puh-tee deh-zhuh-neh*), just as he'd learned to call lunch "déjeuner" and his afternoon snack "goûter" (*ghoo-teh*)—was over, too, and Mother helped Timmie into his coat for it was still cold in the early morning. Daddy called the porter and helped him carry the bags downstairs and load them all on top of the taxi.

Timmie walked down the three flights of stairs with Mother slowly, this time, because he was leaving Paris.

The taxi was waiting in front of the hotel, and Daddy was waiting, too. "Hurry, Tim," he said. "Climb in."

But Timmie wasn't ready to leave Paris yet.

He hung back, and then, just as he was about to get into the taxi, he looked up the street for the last time, and there was Isabelle turning around the corner and running toward him.

"Daddy, wait!" Timmie said. "There's Isabelle."

Daddy looked up the street and saw Isabelle, too.
So he told the taxi driver to wait and then Isabelle
came running up. She shook hands with Mother and
Daddy and then she shook Timmie's hand, the way
she had when she first met him.

"Au revoir," Isabelle said.

Mother and Daddy and Timmie all said, "Au
revoir, Isabelle."

Then, because Isabelle hoped Timmie and Mother
and Daddy would come back to Paris soon she said,
"À Bientôt" (*ah b'yen-toh*).

"À bientôt," Timmie said. "Soon."

And then Isabelle wished them all a pleasant
journey. "Bon voyage" (*bohn vwah-yahzh*).

After that, Mother and Daddy and Timmie got into the taxi and Daddy said, "Gare St. Lazare" (*ghahr san lah-zahr*) and they drove off. But Timmie stared out the back window until Isabelle was out of sight.

As long as he could see her, she was waving to him. "Au revoir, Isabelle," Timmie called out. And he waved, too.

The sun was just coming up as the taxi took them through the narrow streets of the Left Bank, stopping until the trucks moved out of the way, because the streets were too small for them to pass.

They drove to the banks of the Seine, and Timmie, turning around, could see the two towers and the great doors of Notre Dame.

They drove along the Seine, past the bookstalls, still closed for the night, past the shops and the big, gray buildings, until they came to Timmie's very favorite bridge.

There were golden horses guarding it, but the taxi turned onto it, anyway. From the bridge, Timmie looked up and down the Seine, seeing Les Invalides for the last time, and the Eiffel Tower, too.

Across the bridge they drove down broad boulevards, deserted now, for it was early morning. They passed fountains, not yet splashing water, and avenues with gas lamps not yet turned off.

Timmie could see all the way up the Champs-Elysée (*shawn-zeh-lee-zay*) to the Arc de Triomphe, and he saw the other, smaller arch, the Arc du Carrousel (*ark doo car-ooh-zell*) at the end of the Tuileries (*twee-luh-ree*) Gardens as they drove by.

There was no one walking along the streets, yet. But here and there, Timmie and Mother and Daddy passed a worker in his dark blue jacket, sweeping the street with his broom made of twigs.

Then the streets got smaller and the buildings lighter and the sun was on its way up and the sky turned a pale pink.

And at last, and much too soon, the taxi stopped

in front of the sprawling railroad station, the Gare
St. Lazare.

Daddy gave all the luggage to a porter who
loaded it onto a little cart, and they went up the
stairs and through the station and past the gates to
the train that would take them to Le Havre (*luh
hahvr*) and the boat that would take them to New
York.

In the compartment of the train, Timmie stood at
the window, watching the people saying good-by and
the porters bustling back and forth with suitcases
and trunks and the vendors selling magazines and
candies and flowers.

He stood there with his face pressed against the window until the whistle had tooted and the train slipped away, slowly at first, then faster and faster, and the click of the wheels seemed to say "Good-by-good-by-good-by."

They were beyond the city of Paris, beyond the bridges over the Seine, beyond the silver-gray-blue buildings and the houses with the checked curtains at the windows—even out of sight of the Eiffel Tower—before Timmie turned away from the window and curled up on the seat.

He slipped his hand into Mother's and held it very tight. "Mother," he said.

"Yes, Timmie?"

"I feel so funny, Mother."

"Do you, Timmie? Why?"

Timmie shrugged his shoulders, just the way the French do. "I don't know," he said. "It's just that I want to go home, but I want to stay in Paris, too."

"Do you, Timmie?" Mother said again. "That's just the way I feel, too."

Timmie didn't say anything for quite a while. He watched out the window and saw the little pink and blue and orange farmhouses going by. He saw the flowers in the front yards and the pigs in the back. He saw the cabbage growing and the checked curtains at the windows.

"Mother," he said.

"Yes, Timmie?"

But Timmie didn't know what to say. So Mother asked, "What did you like best in Paris, Timmie?"

"The Luxembourg Gardens," Timmie said, right away. Then he changed his mind. "No, I liked the Eiffel Tower just as much. And Les Invalides. And the market place, and the Seine, and the Left Bank and the cafés and the circus, and Isabelle. I just liked everything."

He thought about it some more, and saw tiny villages flash by. He saw churches with pointed steeples, and village squares, and tiny town halls.

"Mother," he said.

"Yes, Timmie?"

"It was all so different, wasn't it?" Timmie remembered the things he'd done and the places he'd gone and the friends he'd made. He remembered all the fun he'd had. "Only it wasn't really different, underneath."

"No," Mother said. "It wasn't really different, underneath."

TIMMIE'S PARIS

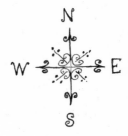

Author VIVIAN WERNER was born in Bellingham, Washington, grew up in Seattle, and received her B.A. degree from Bennington College in Vermont, where she majored in music.

As a free-lance journalist, Mrs. Werner's career has included the writing of radio scripts, advertising copy, and magazine articles as well as books. Her first adult novel, *The Breaking Wave,* published in England, was the British choice for the Prix Formentor of 1961.

In 1953 Mrs. Werner moved to Paris, where her sons Paul and Jan have since grown up completely bilingual. TIMMIE IN PARIS is Mrs. Werner's first book for young readers, and it is based on son Paul's reactions to *his* first trip to Paris (when *he* felt mother's new hat was really a lampshade!).

Artist ELISE PIQUET has been, among other things, an art teacher, an art director for a major publishing house, a magazine illustrator, and an advertising artist. TIMMIE IN PARIS is the first *book* she has illustrated, adding yet another credit to her already impressive list. When not busy at her drawing board, Miss Piquet collects antiques, dotes on her cat, and claims to be an excellent gardener.